MARC BROWN

Arthur's
PERFECT CHRISTMAS

LITTLE, BROWN AND COMPANY

New York ❧ Boston

For Grandma Thora,
for making so many of our
family Christmases perfect

Little, Brown and Company

Time Warner Book Group
1271 Avenue of the Americas, New York, NY 10020
Visit our Web site at www.lb-kids.com

Arthur® is a registered trademark of Marc Brown.

First Paperback Edition 2004

Adapted by Marc Brown from a teleplay by Peter Hirsch

Library of Congress Cataloging-in-Publication Data
Brown, Marc Tolon.
  Arthur's perfect Christmas / Marc Brown — 1st ed.
    p. cm.
    Summary: Even without snow, turkey dinner and a perfect tree, Arthur and his
family and friends have a wonderful Christmas — and Hanukkah — celebration.
  ISBN 0-316-11968-7 (hc) / ISBN 0-316-00130-9 (pb)
  [1. Christmas — Fiction. 2. Aardvark — Fiction. 3. Animals — Fiction.] I. Title.
  PZ7.B81618Arlt 2000
  [E] — dc21   00-035668

HC 10 9 8 7 6 5 4 3 2
PB 10 9 8 7 6 5 4 3 2 1

LAKE

Printed in the United States of America

It was three days before Christmas, and Arthur wanted
everything to be just right.
There would be lots of snow . . .
the perfect tree . . .
and a delicious turkey dinner.

D.W. could only think about all the presents she wanted.
"Arthur!" she said. "Help me write to Santa! I want Tina the
Talking Tabby at the top of the list."

At school the next day, Muffy was very excited.
"My big Christmas party is tomorrow!" she announced.
"Muffy, I told you, I can't —," Francine began.
Muffy wasn't listening. "I forgot to invite George!" She ran off.
"She won't listen!" said Francine.
"Why can't you go?" Arthur asked.
"Every year, we have a family Hanukkah party," Francine said,
"when we light all the candles on the menorah."
"Maybe you should tell her again," Arthur said.
Francine shook her head. "I've told her a million times!"

After school, Arthur invited Buster to go shopping.
"I'm going to bed," said Buster. "My mom woke me up too
early this morning. She thought it was Christmas. It's
happened every year since my parents got divorced. She
cooks special pancakes and gives me all my presents. Then
I tell her it's not Christmas yet and she goes back to bed."
"Weird," Arthur said.
"She's worried that I won't have a good Christmas without
my dad," Buster explained.

At the mall, Arthur found the perfect present for Dad.
"Sorry, we're sold-out," the salesman said. "How about this olive depitter instead?"
"Well, okay," Arthur said.
Arthur found a great present for Mom at another store.
"The little glass bird I broke last summer. Perfect!"

At home, Dad was reading cookbooks.
"I'm making a *real* Christmas dinner," Dad said. "The kind they might have eaten in Bethlehem at the time Jesus was born.

Roast lamb, flat bread, and puls — an ancient Roman dish made with chickpeas."
There goes the *perfect* Christmas dinner, thought Arthur.

The next day, at Muffy's party, everyone was having fun — except Arthur.

"How can it be a perfect Christmas without snow?" said Arthur.

"Well," said the Brain, "no one really knows what day Jesus was born. The holiday is in December probably because that's when the Romans celebrated winter solstice."

"I *still* want snow," said Arthur.

"Gather near, royal subjects!" Muffy announced. "I, the Princess of Christmas, will now give out your presents. The first one is for . . . Francine Frensky!"
Muffy looked for Francine. "I said, 'Francine Frensky!' "
But Francine wasn't there.

The dreidel stopped spinning. "Gimel!" said Francine. "I win again!"

The phone rang. "Francine, it's for you," called her mother.

"WHERE ARE YOU?!" Muffy shouted.

"Muffy," said Francine, "I told you I couldn't come because of our family Hanukkah party."

"But you see your family every day!" Muffy said. "Besides, Hanukkah's not as important as Christmas."

Francine gasped. "Well, it is to me!" She hung up.

Muffy was shocked.

"Buster, wake up," said Arthur.

"Is it Christmas again?" Buster asked. "Time for pancakes?"

"Maybe you and your mom shouldn't have Christmas," said the Brain. "It makes you so tired."

Buster sighed. "But what else can I do?"

"Invent your own holiday," suggested the Brain. "My family celebrates Kwanzaa, and that was invented for African Americans by Dr. Maulana Karenga."

"You could celebrate . . . Baxter Day!" said Arthur.

Buster wasn't so sure.

When he got home, Arthur couldn't believe his eyes.
"*That* doesn't look like a Christmas tree!" Arthur said.
"Yes it does!" said D.W. "It's beautiful!"

"I wanted something *normal*," said Arthur. "Not unicorns and trolls!"

"You can decorate the rest of the tree," Mom said, "just the way you want."

There goes the perfect tree, thought Arthur.

Later, Arthur wrapped all his gifts and put them under the tree.
"Mom is going to be so surprised!" he said.
D.W. came in with cookies, milk, and a bucket.

"For Santa," she said. "Now help me fill this pail with water."
"Water?" Arthur asked.
"For the reindeer, silly," said D.W.

Arthur had just climbed into bed when he heard a loud crash outside.
"Oops!" said a voice.
"Uncle Fred! I thought you were going to Florida," said Arthur.
"I thought I'd drop off your presents first," Uncle Fred said, "and my truck just died! Sorry about the fence. Clumsy me!"

Arthur remembered how Uncle Fred had broken Mom's tea set last Christmas.

"You're welcome to stay here," Mom said. "Rory, too."

Arthur heard barks and growls from the living room.

Rory and Pal were fighting over Mom's present.

"Let go of that!" shouted Arthur.

The box went flying through the air.

Arthur made a wild dive and caught the box before it hit the floor. "Whew!"

He decided to put the gift in a safe place.

The next morning, D.W. woke everyone up.
"Arthur, wake up, it's Christmas!" she cried.

"Mommy, Daddy, it's Christmas, wake up, Christmas is here!"

D.W. stopped in the hall.
"*Santa?*"
"It's Uncle Fred," said Arthur.
"*Uncle Fred is Santa?*" asked D.W.

"Guess what, Mom!" Buster said. "It's Christmas!"

"Are you sure?" she asked.

"Yep, December twenty-fifth," Buster answered.

"Time for presents! Time for pancakes!" said his mother.

Muffy counted her presents. "Thirty-seven! The biggest
Christmas ever! Wait till Francine hears —"
Then she remembered that they weren't speaking to each other.
Muffy opened her new makeup kit and looked in the mirror.
"I don't really need makeup. But Francine might like it."
But Francine wasn't her friend anymore.

Muffy looked around the room at her new games, puzzles, dolls, train set, and miniature submarine.

"Daddy," she said, "my gifts aren't fun if I can't share them with Francine!"

Her father thought for a moment. "Let's go for a drive, Muffin. Maybe that'll take your mind off things."

Mrs. Baxter watched nervously as Buster opened his first gift.

"CyberCod!" exclaimed Buster.

"I'm sorry, we can return it," said his mother.

"Why?" Buster asked.

"You already have it," she said. "I just saw it in your room."

"No," Buster explained, "that's TechnoTrout."

Just then, Buster smelled smoke. "The pancakes!"
They dashed into the kitchen. "They're burnt!" said
Buster's mother. "I'm sorry!"
"It's okay, Mom," said Buster. "I like them kind of
brown ... er, black."

"Let's open presents," said D.W. "I bet Tina is in this one!"
"Wait! Don't start without me!" Arthur ran upstairs to get
Mom's gift.
He reached up into the closet, but he was so excited that . . .
CRACK!
Arthur quickly opened the box. The glass bird was broken.
"Oh, no," said Arthur sadly.

Uncle Fred came upstairs to find Arthur.

"Everybody's waiting — what's wrong?"

"I broke Mom's present," said Arthur. "It was the perfect gift and now it's ruined!"

"That's a shame," said Uncle Fred. "But Christmas is more than just presents, you know."

"That's what grown-ups always say," Arthur said.

Uncle Fred looked at Arthur's gift card.

"Well, the day's not over yet!" he said. "Let's go back down."

Francine answered the door. "Muffy?"
Muffy took a deep breath. "I'm sorry about what I said, but you're my best friend and the party was important to me."
"Come in," Francine said. "I want to explain why Hanukkah is important to me."

She showed Muffy the menorah. "On the last night of Hanukkah, all my relatives come to our house. After our potluck dinner, we say prayers together and then my father lights all the candles. It really makes me feel like I'm part of something special."

"I'm so sorry," said Muffy. "I should have listened to you."

"You forgot the best family tradition of all," said Mr. Frensky.

"What's that?" Muffy asked.

"Going to the movies!" Francine answered. "Come on!"

"Another Veginator!" said Dad. "That makes four!"

D.W. had one present left. "I know what this is!" She tore off the wrapping paper with one swipe. "It has to be . . . " She ripped the box open.

". . . a duck?" D.W. looked confused.

"Not just any duck!" Mom said. "A duck that says four thousand words!"

"Can it say 'Meow'?" asked D.W.

"Well, no . . . ," Mom said. "Are you upset?"

"No . . . ," said D.W. "But . . . I WANTED TINA THE TALKING TABBY! OH, SANTA, HOW COULD YOU? THIS IS THE WORST CHRISTMAS EVER!"

D.W. stomped around the room and accidentally stepped on the duck.

"Hello!" it said. "I'm Quackers the Talking Duck!"
D.W. picked up the duck and squeezed it.
"I love you!" it said. "Do you love me?"
"Hey," said D.W., "you're kind of cute." She squeezed it again.
"Quack-a-doodle-do!" said Quackers.
D.W. giggled.

QUACKERS

Arthur wished he had a gift for his mother.

"Mom," he began, "I have to tell you something—"

"Wait!" said Uncle Fred. "There's one more present! The card says, 'To Mom. Love, Arthur.'"

"It does?" Arthur said.

"Oh, Arthur, thank you!" said Mom. "It's the tea set that Fred broke last Christmas!"

"Better keep it away from me!" joked Uncle Fred.

Arthur didn't know what to say.

At the Pancake Palace, Buster's mother checked her list. "Everything's planned," she said. "After this it's Penguins on Ice—"

"Mom—," Buster began.

"Then we'll rush home so I can start the roast and make the pudding—"

"Mom!"

"Then we'll watch the TV special. Then we'll—"

"MOM!"

Mrs. Baxter looked up. "Yes, dear?"

Buster took a deep breath. "Maybe Christmas can be a day where we just *relax*."

"Relax?" said Buster's mother. "On Christmas?"

"We could sleep late, and eat breakfast and open our presents whenever we wanted. At night we could just sit outside and look at the stars. And we wouldn't even have to call it Christmas. It could be our own holiday — Baxter Day."

Buster's mother smiled. "Baxter Day! I love it."

Everyone at the Reads' house was stuffed, except for Arthur.
"Dinner was great!" said Arthur. "More halvah, please."
"Arthur, I love this olive depitter!" said Dad. "It's so useful!"
"Good news!" said Uncle Fred. "My truck is fixed, so Rory
and I will be going to Florida after all."
Arthur and Uncle Fred went to get his suitcase.
"The tea set was *your* present for Mom, wasn't it?" Arthur
asked him.
"Yes," Uncle Fred answered, "but it was a lot nicer coming
from you."

Everyone waved good-bye.
As Grandpa Dave backed out of the driveway, he hit the
other half of the fence. It fell over with a crash.
"Oops!" called Grandpa Dave. "Sorry!"
Mom sighed. "Like father, like son."

Later, when Arthur went outside, he was amazed.
"It's snowing!" he shouted. "This *is* a perfect Christmas!"

"Arthur Read!" D.W. yelled. "You'd better come inside before you catch puh-monia!"

"Do you still like Santa?" Arthur asked. "He didn't give you what you wanted."

"Of course," said D.W. "He knew I'd like Quackers better than Tina!"

She hugged Quackers.

"Quicky-quacky-doodle-do! You love me and I love you!"

"He can say four thousand words and I want you to hear all of them," said D.W.

"Oh, no!" Arthur groaned.